This Rising Moon book belongs to:

There was a Coyote Who Swallowed a Flea

by Jennifer Ward

Illustrated by Steve Gray

rising moon

www.risingmoonbooks.com

www.risingmoonbooks.com

Composed in the United States of America
Printed in China

Edited by Theresa Howell
Designed by David Alston

FIRST IMPRESSION 2007
ISBN 13: 978-0-87358-898-0
ISBN 10: 0-87358-898-3

11   10   09   08   07   5   4   3   2   1

Library of Congress Cataloging-in-Publication Data

Ward, Jennifer, 1963-
    There was a coyote who swallowed a flea / by Jennifer Ward ; illustrated by Steve Gray.
        p. cm.
    Summary: Set in the desert southwest, this variation on the traditional,
    cumulative rhyme looks at the consequences of a coyote's strange diet.
        ISBN-13: 978-0-87358-898-0 (hardcover : alk. paper)
        ISBN-10: 0-87358-898-3 (hardcover : alk. paper)
        1. Folk songs, English—England—Texts.   [1. Folk songs.
        2. Non-sense verses.]   I. Gray, Steve, 1950-   , ill. II. Title.
    PZ8.3.W2135The 2006
    782.42162'2100268—dc22
    [E]
                                2006007440

For my sister, Cathy,
who kept singing "the song."
—J.W.

To the sweetest girl in the world,
Cindy Morningstar...Gray!
—G.G.

there was a coyote

Who swallowed a flea,

Plucked from his knee, that tickly flea.
Yippee-o-ki-yee!

There was a coyote who swallowed a lizard.
It slipped and it slithered right down to his gizzard.

He swallowed the lizard to catch the flea,
Plucked from his knee, that tickly flea.

Yippee-O-Ki-Yee!

there was a coyote

who swallowed a snake.
It tasted like steak, that rattling snake.

He swallowed the snake to catch the lizard.
He swallowed the lizard to catch the flea,
Plucked from his knee, that tickly flea.
Yippee-o-Ki-Yee!

There was a coyote
who swallowed a bird.

that's what
I heard!
He swallowed
a bird.

He swallowed the bird to catch the snake.
He swallowed the snake to catch the lizard.
He swallowed the lizard to catch the flea,
Plucked from his knee, that tickly flea.

YiPPee-o-Ki-Yee!

There was a coyote who swallowed a chile.
Call him silly to swallow a chile!

He swallowed the chile to season the bird.
He swallowed the bird to catch the snake.
He swallowed the snake to catch the lizard.
He swallowed the lizard to catch the flea,
Plucked from his knee, that tickly flea.

Yippee-o-ki-yee!

there was a coyote

who swallowed a cactus.
It takes lots of practice to swallow a cactus!

He swallowed the cactus to go with the chile.

He swallowed the chile to season the bird.

He swallowed the bird to catch the snake.

He swallowed the snake to catch the lizard.

He swallowed the lizard to catch the flea,

Plucked from his knee, that tickly flea.

Yippee-o-ki-yee!

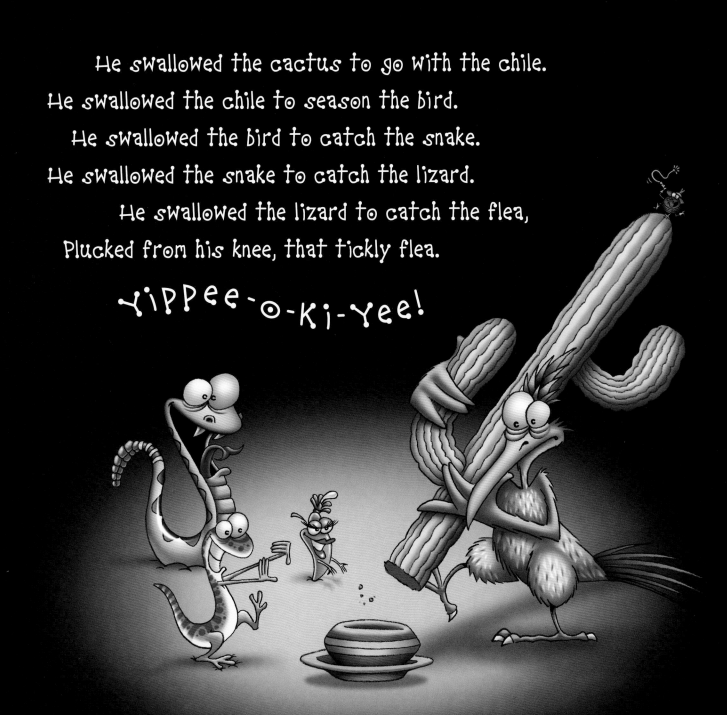

there was a coyote who swallowed a hat,

A ten gallon hat in ten seconds flat!

He swallowed the hat right after the cactus.
He swallowed the cactus to go with the chile.
He swallowed the chile to season the bird.
He swallowed the bird to catch the snake.
He swallowed the snake to catch the lizard.
He swallowed the lizard to catch the flea,
Plucked from his knee, that tickly flea.

Yippee-o-ki-yee!

There was a coyote
   who swallowed a boot.
What a hoot
   to swallow a boot!

He swallowed the boot to stomp the hat.
He swallowed the hat right after the cactus.
He swallowed the cactus to go with the chile.
He swallowed the chile to season the bird.
He swallowed the bird to catch the snake.
He swallowed the snake to catch the lizard.
He swallowed the lizard to catch the flea,
Plucked from his knee, that tickly flea.

Yippee-o-Ki-Yee!

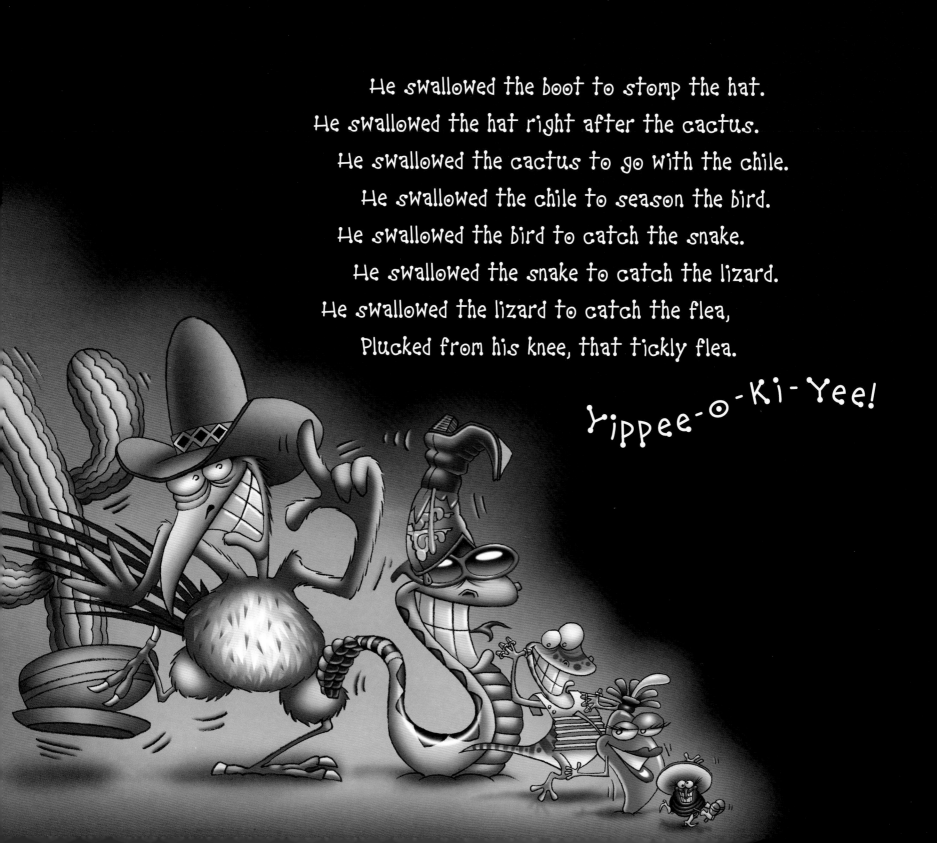

There was a coyote who swallowed a bull.

You'd think he was full after gulping that bull!
He swallowed the bull to squash the boot.
He swallowed the boot to stomp the hat.
He swallowed the hat right after the cactus.
He swallowed the cactus to go with the chile.
He swallowed the chile to season the bird.
He swallowed the bird to catch the snake.
He swallowed the snake to catch the lizard.
He swallowed the lizard to catch the flea,
Plucked from his knee, that tickly flea.

Yippee-o-ki-yee?

There was a coyote who swallowed the moon.

Burp!

Is breakfast soon?